Praise for *Wo*

'The nine stories that make *1*
in the imagination like a *st*
the familiar gospel *narrativ*
wealth of biblical knowledge,
often spoken over by *loude* *voices. She spots the gaps in the*
biblical accounts where much is possible, and where we, too,
might imagine our own stories finding their place.'

CATHERINE FOX
Novelist and lecturer in creative writing

'Once more Paula Gooder offers us her extraordinary blend of deep
scholarship and empathetic story-telling. She allows us to see both the
prophetic foreshadowing and the miraculous reality of the Incarnation
through the eyes of the women, both sung and unsung, whose lives were
transformed and woven into the story of God's grace and our redemption.
Ally Barrett's vivid and compelling paintings combine with Paula's
story-telling to bring it all to life. It's not just that we feel as though we
were there as we read these stories, but that by the end we know through
these stories, that the love of God at the heart of them, is there for us.'

MALCOLM GUITE
Poet and priest

'The combination of Paula Gooder's weaving together of biblical
narratives and creative imagination, together with Ally Barrett's
captivating illustrations can't fail but draw the reader in to a fresh
encounter with familiar seasonal themes. Well known figures mingle with
newcomers, inviting us to ponder the timeless mysteries of faith, all set
sensitively within the culture and context into which Jesus was born.'

BISHOP GULI FRANCIS-DEHQANI

Paula Gooder is a writer and biblical scholar whose many books make her expertise accessible to a wide readership. They include *Lydia* and *Phoebe* which relate in story form the lives of significant New Testament figures, and the *Biblical Exploration* series. Paula is also one of the editors of the *Pilgrim* course. She is Canon Chancellor of St Paul's Cathedral, London.

Ally Barrett has worked in theological education, university chaplaincy and parish ministry and enjoys working at the intersection of creativity, faith, wellbeing and sustainability. She is the author of several books and dozens of hymns.

Women of the Nativity

An Advent and Christmas journey in nine stories

Paula Gooder

with illustrations by Ally Barrett

Church House Publishing

Text © Paula Gooder 2024
Illustrations © Ally Barrett 2024

Church House Publishing
Church House
27 Great Smith Street
London SW1P 3AZ

Published 2024 by Church House Publishing
Reprinted 2025

British Library Cataloguing in Publication Data

A catalogue record for this book is available from the British Library

ISBN 978 1 78140 460 7

EU GPSR Authorised Representative
LOGOS EUROPE, 9 rue Nicolas Poussin, 17000,
LA ROCHELLE, France
E-mail: Contact@logoseurope.eu

Design and typesetting by www.penguinboy.net

Printed and bound in Poland by Opolgraf Printing House

Contents

NOTES AND RESOURCES

Introduction

THIS BOOK, like its companion *Women of Holy Week* published in 2022, consists of nine imagined stories all from the perspective of women.

Here, as in that book, I was keen to look again at well-known and well-loved stories of the Bible, though this time these stories focus not on the end of Jesus' earthly life but on its beginning. They take us through Advent to the glorious celebration of Jesus' birth and onwards into the Christmas season. As we trace this old, old story I wanted to ask the question of what it was like to be there and what it might have felt like to be a woman who observed these world-changing events.

Some of the women in this book (Sarah, Huldah, Elizabeth, Mary and Anna) are clearly named in the text of the Bible. Others of them existed but are not mentioned in the Bible itself, key among them are Mariamne II, Herod the Great's wife at the time of the birth of Jesus. Others still, like Abigail, Rachel and Shiphrah, are fictional, but someone like them might have existed.

On the four Sundays before Christmas, a candle is lit on the Advent wreath. Each candle is associated with different characters in the preparation for the birth of Jesus. The first is connected with the Patriarchs (and the Matriarchs) – people like Abraham and Sarah, Isaac and Rebekah, Jacob, Leah and Rachel. The second invites us to reflect on the Prophets; the third and fourth, John the Baptist and Mary respectively. I used these four themes as the springboard for my first four stories. The rest of the stories are all associated with the key feasts commemorated in the Church's calendar between Christmas Day and The Presentation of Christ in the Temple (Candlemas).

With each story I have provided (at the back of the book) one or more Bible passages that can be read alongside the stories, and some questions to prompt reflection and conversation. In addition, for each story I have provided a few notes which you might find helpful and which might aid you in your own inhabiting of the events described.

We have become so used to the Christmas stories and associate them so strongly in our minds with a 'child-friendly' festival that it can be easy to forget the reality that lies behind them. Looking at the events through the eyes of women makes the bleakness of the stories hard to ignore. These are stories of women shunned by society because they couldn't have children or, in the case of Mary, because they became pregnant outside of marriage. They remind us of the courage needed to speak out and of the unsettling, disturbing consequences of God's favour. They tell of the precarious nature of women's lives in a world in which they had little, if any, power. They also speak of the God who walks alongside us through it all bringing courage and hope when and where it is most needed.

Looking at the stories of Christmas through the eyes of women reminds us that these are not just 'nice stories for the children'. They are stories that bring us face to face with the harsh realities of life, but also with the God who loved the world so much that he sent Jesus, the Word made flesh, to live with us. As I write this introduction at the start of 2024, I hold in my heart all those around the world whose experience overlaps so tragically with the lives of some of those mentioned in the Christmas story, those mourning the loss of their children or other loved ones, of their homes and livelihoods, of their safety and peace of mind, and praying that Jesus, Immanuel, might bring them the light and peace of his presence.

The stories of Christmas present life as it really is, but also as God yearns for it to be. A life shot through with the light of Christ, which shines and shines and never stops. A life permeated by the love of the God, who knows us inside and out. I hope that these stories help you to see afresh a vision of the world as God yearns for it to be and to know, as though for first time, the wonder of God with us, the Word made flesh.

Paula Gooder

Epiphany 2024

About
the Paintings

Ally Barrett

T HE STORY OF THE INCARNATION is far bigger than the Christmas story. From the time of Sarah and Abraham's journeys to Simeon and Anna in the Temple, the events we recall between Advent Sunday and Candlemas span some two thousand years. In these paintings I looked for ways to draw out this larger narrative by creating some visual coherence between them, allowing the ripples created by each story to intersect and let the paintings and stories speak to one another, just as Paula has done through the words.

Most obviously, what begins as Sarah's shawl in the first painting appears in all nine images. An extended conversation with a friend, Hester Lees-Jeffries (who works on Renaissance literature and material culture) led me to explore using a piece of cloth for this recurring visual 'hook' to reflect the cloth that we associate with birth – the swaddling bands, and the towels that appear in the middle painting (the Nativity itself) and because until very recently cloth would have been used and re-used over and over, made and mended by many (women's) hands over years, even generations.

The cloth of birth is never (biblically, at least) far away from the cloth of the grave. Along the way, the cloth becomes the towel with which Joseph dries Mary's swollen feet (The Fourth Sunday of Advent), prefiguring the events of Maundy Thursday, pointing to Joseph's servanthood as well as to Jesus' own.

At Holy Innocents it is a heartbreakingly empty baby blanket, which retains the scent of the child for his mother to breathe in. And at Epiphany it offers a scrap of comfort against the cold of the night and the horror of Herod's rage, and probably covers the other bruises, too.

In Sarah's painting, the very tree under which she laughs at the idea of being the mother of a nation is shaped like the promise: branching into two, and two again, and eventually into twelve. And the ram that looks up at her somehow knows that it, too, will have a role to play in that promise (Genesis 22). The paintings for Rachel (Holy Innocents) and Elizabeth (Naming and Circumcision) mirror each other in their composition: the mothers of the children lost (by such as Eve and Bathsheba), and the mothers of children given (to Sarah, Hannah, and more).

Y NAME IS SARAH. Or at least it is now. A few months back Abram burst into the tent, his eyes shining like they always did when he met God.

'The Lord spoke to me,' he said.

I sighed wearily. 'Again?'

In my experience 'the Lord' appearing to Abram meant nothing but disruption and dashed hopes. 'What was it this time?'

'We have new names!' Abram declared. 'Mine is Abraham. And yours is Sarah.'

'What was wrong with our old names?'

I'd got used to Sarai after nearly eighty-nine years of using it, and, in any case, I'd always liked it when Abram called me 'Sarai – my princess'.

You might be wondering about my lack of enthusiasm. As I tell you about it, even I wince at my grumpiness.

But this God keeps messing with my life.

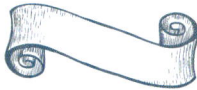

IT ALL BEGAN NEARLY twenty-five years ago now. By then we'd already moved from Ur. I loved it there. The city was huge, the buildings grand. It was right on the coast, and our house looked out over the Euphrates. I would fall to sleep each night soothed into rest by the sound of the gentle lapping of the waves.

Then Haran died. Haran was Abram's younger brother. Terah, their father, was devastated. For months he barely spoke a word, until one day he stood in the grand entrance way to our beautiful house and declared that we were moving; all of us, without delay.

'Where are we going?' I asked Abram later, hoping he'd say to another house round the corner.

'To Canaan,' he replied.

'Where's *that*?' I asked.

He shrugged, 'Somewhere across the desert.'

'But why?' I wailed. 'I like it here.'

Abram sighed, 'You'll get used to it.'

I didn't. I didn't even have chance to. We trailed across the desert for months. We in the women's tent had a lot to say about the heat and the distance and the constant travelling and the discomfort and the tents. Oh, the tents! They were so hot and so noisy. How I yearned for our house by the sea, with its cool breezes and beautiful vistas.

Onwards we trudged through the desert, until at last, we came to a place called Haran.

'Here we are,' said Terah sinking down wearily. 'This is where we stay.'

Later I asked Abram about it.

'I thought we were going to Canaan? Is this Canaan? And isn't it weird to live in a place with the same name as your dead brother?'

Abram smiled at me gently. 'Have patience, my princess, we'll know in time. And the name of this place is pronounced *Charran* not *Haran*. Not the same at all.'

A bubble of laughter started in my belly and worked

its way upwards. Laughter has always come easily to me. As a child, my mother would find me playing by the sea by following the sound of my laughter. The laughter never left me, but the older I got, the more jaded it became. More often than not, these days, by the time the laughter emerged from my mouth it had turned into a cynical 'ha' – a far cry from the ripples of joy of my youth.

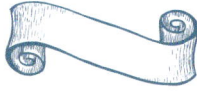

A FEW MONTHS LATER, Terah also died. A few days after that was the first time this God appeared to Abram. Abram burst into the tent his eyes shining.

'The Lord spoke to me!'

'Which lord?' I asked surprised.

'The Lord God!'

'Which lord god?' I was used to many different gods. In Ur we had worshipped Nannar, god of the moon. When we travelled, we'd brought with us our household gods. The women we spoke to in Charan had told us of Astarte and Haddad. There were a lot to choose from.

'No,' he said, '*The … Lord … God.*'

I had no idea what he was saying and was about to change the subject to the hole in the roof of the tent that would need mending before the rains came, when Abram added, 'He told us to go from our country.'

'We already have,' I said – sounding acerbic even to my ear.

' … And from our kindred and from our father's house,' continued Abram, as though I hadn't spoken.

'Where to this time?'

'To a place that he will show us.'

'How will we know this place? Couldn't we wait here until he tells us?'

'No, my princess,' he said fondly, 'of course we can't. We have to follow. Have faith, it will be fun.'

I doubted this and was in the middle of rolling my eyes at the thought of wandering about waiting for some kind of god to tell us to stop, when he continued:

'And I will be the father of a great nation.'

This was too much. That familiar bubble of laughter formed in my belly again.

'There's a bit of a problem, don't you think? You are old. I am old. Where precisely is this nation coming from?'

'The Lord God has promised,' said Abram steadfastly. 'We must have faith.'

I looked at him and shook my head. I didn't know this God he was talking about. He might have appeared to Abram, but he hadn't appeared to me. I did, however, have faith in my gentle, thoughtful husband – and hoped that would be enough.

THAT WAS TWENTY-FIVE YEARS AGO. Twenty-five long years of wandering and hoping, hoping and wandering. At what point, I often asked myself, do you give up? When do you realize that the promise you believed in is never coming true? I asked Abram this many times over the years.

'Just have faith,' he would reply.

I had asked him again a few hours ago. 'Just have faith,' he said, as he always did. And I screamed at him, screamed out all my years of dashed hopes and despair. He hoped for a great nation to bear his name. I just hoped for a tiny human being, the tangible expression of the aching love in my heart. He patted my cheek sadly and went to sit at the entrance of the tent. He sat with his back to me. The silence between us palpable. After twenty-five years of hopes stretched thin and dreams destroyed, what more can there be to say?

He was still sitting there a few moments ago, when I saw him stand suddenly and heard his voice greeting some strangers. There was a stranger – no, three strangers – outside. I heard Abraham shout commands and felt our camp stir into action as the women of the camp ran backwards and forwards, preparing an impromptu feast for our guests. I was too heartsick to join them. So I stayed in the tent, alone with my bitterness and despair.

I was sitting with my head in my hands when I heard my name. One of the strangers was asking for me by name. It was so odd that it drew me to the tent entrance, where Abraham had sat a little while before. I was just in time to hear the stranger say, 'Your wife will bear a son.'

That familiar bubble of laughter formed in my belly again and burst out of me, more like a snort, this time, than a laugh.

'Why did Sarah laugh?' The stranger asked Abraham.

Why indeed? I thought to myself. Why would I not laugh? The years of waiting. The heartbreak and sorrow. Our dearest hopes – mine and Abraham's – raised and dashed so often. If I didn't laugh I'd weep, and, once started, may never stop.

But his question frightened me. How could he possibly have known that I laughed? There is no way he could have heard. The noise I'd made was barely audible even to me. So I denied it.

'I didn't laugh,' I said, hoping to persuade him that whatever he thought he'd heard was the creaking of our well-travelled tent.

'No, but you did laugh,' he said looking right at me.

I found the courage to raise my eyes to meet his. I expected to see in them challenge or derision or, worst of all, pity. But all I saw was love. His eyes brimmed with compassion and understanding. It was almost as though he'd heard my cries and knew all the pain and the sorrow, the weariness and the heartache of those long, long years.

He turned to go with his two companions, Abraham joining them and pointing out the way to Sodom on the far horizon. And I felt that laugh again. 'I did laugh,' I whispered to myself. The laugh hovered for a moment and then travelled back down again, warming my heart as it went. It settled at last in my belly. My body felt somehow different. There was an odd taste in my mouth. My breasts – which for years had sagged ever downwards – felt suddenly full, even tender.

I placed my hand wonderingly on my belly. And for the first time in years, I allowed the laughter to bubble joyfully through me. I was still laughing on and off when Abraham returned from guiding the visitors on their way.

So NINE MONTHS LATER, when the midwives placed the tiny bundle of life in my arms, there was only one name for him: Isaac. It means laughter.

The stranger was right, I did laugh.

The Second Sunday of Advent
(The Prophets)
HULDAH'S STORY

The candle on the Advent wreath for Advent 2 reminds us of the Prophets. Only a few women are identified as prophets in the Bible, one of the most important is Huldah.

M Y NAME IS HULDAH. I am a prophet. People usually look surprised when they hear this.

'You don't look like a prophet,' they say.

I used to ask them what a prophet looks like, bristling slightly in response. But now my nephew Jeremiah has grown up, I know what they mean. Jeremiah looks like a prophet. His hair is wild, his beard ragged but nevertheless impressive, his gaze as fierce as his spirit. He looks like a prophet.

'You should be pleased,' my husband Shallum would say to me. 'I don't think you really want to look like a prophet. Do you?'

I would shrug and say nothing. It felt too complicated to explain. It's hard enough to get people to listen to you when you're telling them something they don't want to hear, but even harder when you don't look like they think you should.

JEREMIAH HADN'T ALWAYS LOOKED like a prophet. When he was a boy, he was small for his age – quiet and well dressed. His hair neat, his clothes tidy. He came to me when his head barely reached my shoulder. He came to me because he knew I was a prophet, and that knowledge was as natural to him as the knowledge that my husband Shallum was his uncle and I was his aunt.

'Aunt Huldah,' he said. 'The word of the Lord came to me.'

I turned my full attention on him because, as he knew so well, the word of the Lord came to me, too. I would feel it first at the top of my head. A tingling, prickly sensation, then it would flow through the whole of my body until words would form unbidden, and I would have to speak whether I wanted to or not.

'Couldn't you just keep quiet?' my husband Shallum would ask sometimes.

'No,' I would respond. 'No more than the wind can stop blowing or the sun can stop shining.'

Knowing this, I turned my full attention to my small nephew.

'What did God say?' I asked, my heart in my mouth.

The calling to be a prophet is hard and my heart ached for my beloved nephew, whose eyes shone so brightly at my shoulder. 'God said that I was appointed a prophet to the nations.'

'But you are so small!' The words tumbled out before I could stop them.

Jeremiah grinned at me. 'That's what I said. But God touched my mouth and said he'd give me words. He paused. His forehead wrinkled with worry. 'Do you think the people will listen to me?'

I was about to pat his arm and say what we often say to children, to shrink the full terror of the world into a size that they can deal with. But then I stopped. If God had called him, young as he was, to be a prophet who was I to withhold the truth from him?

'Beloved,' I said. 'The word of the Lord is rarely welcome. Deep truth is unsettling. Most people fit their lives around what troubles them least. I can't remember the last time anyone was pleased when I spoke the word of the Lord to them.'

He nodded, gravely. 'They'll hate me, won't they?'

'Sometimes,' I replied. 'Most of the time they'll ignore you.'

AT FIRST, WHEN JEREMIAH DECLARED the word of the Lord, he looked tentative and a little hesitant, as if he expected people to take no notice of him. So they did exactly that. They either ignored him entirely or ruffled his hair and told him to run along. As he grew, though, he grew in boldness. Today he is the fiercest person I know. Some might say too fierce. Today people take no notice, not because he is hesitant, but because he frightens them. His vehemence makes his message too uncomfortable to hear.

I wonder sometimes what the perfect way to deliver the word of God is. Delivered too gently, and people find it easy to take no notice; delivered too forcefully, and they erect barriers to protect themselves from the blast.

I was mulling on this when Shallum arrived unexpectedly in our tiny home just north of the Temple.

Priests I knew by sight but not by name trailed in after him, filling the tiny space with an anxious presence. They all spoke at once, their voices jarring against each other, until one, who announced himself to be Hilkiah the High Priest, took charge.

'Allow me,' he said, and explained what had happened.

King Josiah had become concerned about the general disrepair of the Temple – there was much muttering and nodding of heads at this. I knew from Shallum that the one thing that united Priests and Levites alike was the parlous state of the Temple. It had been neglected for so long that you had to pick a careful route through the Temple courts, around the fallen masonry and general debris that had built up over the years. I suspected from the looks on the Priests' faces that Josiah had not arrived at his newfound concern about the state of the Temple entirely by himself.

Josiah, apparently, had sent them into the Temple storehouses to retrieve the tax money. This detail prompted another flurry of discussion between the priests about how much money they had expected to find. It was clear that there was less than there should have been. It was also clear that this was because King Josiah's predecessors had dipped into the Temple treasury whenever they wanted to. It was even more clear that even though everyone knew this, no one had any intention of saying so to the King.

I was confused. Were they hoping that I would say what they lacked the courage to say for themselves? Surely, they knew I didn't just say difficult things to order?

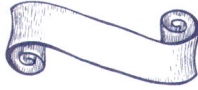

I SHUDDERED AT THE MEMORY of the times I stood in the Temple courts during the reigns of Manasseh and Amon and proclaimed the word of the Lord. Time and time again I had condemned their actions. Time and time again they had ignored me, except for the times when they had imprisoned me or had me beaten. But I had condemned them because the word of the Lord had come to me, not because someone had asked me to.

'I do not like you,' King Manasseh had said on one occasion. 'You always prophesy evil against me and never good. These prophets I like.' He gesticulated behind him to a group of harassed and anxious looking young men. 'You,' he said pointing to one of them, 'what does the Lord have to say today?'

The young man had turned pale. 'That you are a great and righteous king, O King,' he stammered.

I had stood my ground and looked him firmly in the eye.

'Persuading someone to prophesy something good about you is easy. What is harder is believing it yourself.'

He had broken my gaze then and looked away nervously.

'I can have you killed, you know.'

'I do know,' I had replied, my legs quivering with fear. 'Kill all the prophets you like, but God will still speak. You know that.'

I SIGHED. I HAD HOPED those days were over. Standing up to those in power had to be done when the word of the Lord came, but it never got easier. My gaze fell on some dusty scrolls clutched by Hilkiah.

'What are those?' I asked.

'These are why we came,' Hilkiah answered. 'We found them when we were counting out the money and Josiah wanted to ask you about them.'

I slumped with relief. Maybe they hadn't come to ask me to speak hard words to the King after all.

I unrolled the first one.

'These are the words which Moses spoke to all Israel,' I read.

I read and read, the room resounding with the words as though Moses himself were here speaking to us. After a couple of hours, I neared the end: 'Never since has there arisen a prophet in Israel like Moses, whom the Lord knew face to face.'

Silence filled the room. If only, I thought, I had known God face to face, like Moses had. If I had, maybe this job of speaking out would feel easier. I felt the familiar stirring of the Spirit and as I spoke tears poured down my face.

'Disaster is coming,' I said. 'It's coming on us all. We turned our backs on God and his ways, and his anger will rain down on us.'

Hilkiah looked at me, his face calculating. 'I think you can tell the King that yourself.'

Telling the King of his imminent punishment by God – and possible death – was not a task he relished. My flicker of hope, that they hadn't come to make me do the task they didn't want to do, had been very short-lived.

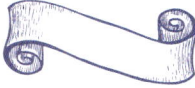

But God continued to speak.

'Wait,' I said, 'There's more. God says that because Josiah listened and repented, he will not see the disaster. He will die in peace.'

'Maybe I'll tell him myself,' said Hilkiah his tone lightening. 'He's a young man. Maybe it won't happen in our lifetimes.' He smiled as though I had delivered a great gift.

'I'm not sure that's what the message is,' I said.

My husband Shullum spoke for the first time.

'My grandfather Harhas kept the wardrobe during the time of the great King Hezekiah. Isaiah prophesied destruction to him. My grandfather told me Hezekiah used to report the prophesy and add, "Why not, if there will be peace and security in my days?" But I've always wondered what would have happened if he had done more then.'

Hilkiah shrugged. 'Peace and security in my days sounds good to me.'

'But what about the future?' Shallum asked, his face full of concern. 'What about our children and our children's children?'

'Let's just worry about today,' said Hilkiah. The Priests around the room nodded their agreement. 'We need to be careful not to unsettle people.'

I stood, suddenly overwhelmed by the urgency facing us. My heart full with the need to make him understand.

'You must make Josiah listen. We must act now. Perhaps we can still make a difference.'

Hilkiah sniffed. 'We came to you for gentle words. If we'd wanted discomfort we'd have gone to your nephew, Jeremiah. You prophets are all the same. We came for reassurance not discouragement.'

'But you will tell him?' I asked. 'You will make Josiah understand?'

'Of course,' he said, though his nose twitched as though he was passing the rubbish dump outside the city walls.

He turned and swept out of the house, the four other priests scurrying to keep up with him.

'Do you think he will tell Josiah?' I asked Shallum.

'Possibly,' he answered. 'But all you can do is speak the message given to you. You can't make people listen.'

He paused. 'I'll tell you one thing, though.'

'What?' I asked.

The third candle on the Advent wreath is for John the Baptist. This story is about the annunciation of John's birth. The later story for the feast of the Naming and Circumcision of Jesus also focuses on Elizabeth and John the Baptist and could be read for Advent 3 instead.

M Y NAME IS ABIGAIL. My husband, Eleazar is a priest. As I tell you this, I feel myself standing taller, full of pride. We've been married for five years now, but last month Eleazar turned twenty, so at last he can serve as a priest in the Temple. He's been there since he was a young boy, watching what was going on, learning what to do, studying the Torah and gaining all the knowledge he needed to be a priest. But he couldn't actually be a priest because he was too young.

This year, for the first time, he isn't too young. Now his time has come. He is in the division of Abijah and this week is their week of service in the Temple. Eleazar was happy and so am I. I was so excited that I came to Jerusalem with him from the hill county.

'You don't need to come,' he kept on saying. 'Wives don't usually come. Wait till one of the big festivals, then come.'

But I begged him, and in the end he gave in. I got the feeling that much as he wouldn't admit it – and much as he pretended embarrassment at having his wife trail after him – he would be pleased to have me there. He warned me that I shouldn't get too excited, though, as his duties wouldn't be much this time. As the most junior priest, his would be the most menial jobs: fetching and carrying, cleaning down the blood from the altar so the stench didn't get too overpowering, getting the incense ready for burning in the Holy Place. That kind of thing.

'Only …' he said.

'Only what?' I asked, sensing the hint of something in his tone.

'If God favours me ...'

'Yes,' I said, 'If you God favours you, then … ?'

'The lot might fall on me to go into the Holy Place to offer the incense.'

I clapped my hands in delight.

'Inside the Holy Place? Will you be next to the Holy of Holies? Will you tell me what the Temple veil looks like? I've heard the cherubim on it are huge, and the pattern beautiful. Oh, if only God would show us favour, how great would that be? I've heard …'

Eleazar placed his finger over his lips. 'Too much, dear one,' he said, gently. 'Too many questions. Let's just see what happens.'

WE TRAVELLED THE NEXT WEEK to Jerusalem. On the journey, I peppered Eleazar with questions. He would laugh and answer some of them and then, when my curiosity got too much he would place his finger softly on his lips to indicate I should stop.

We quickly settled into a routine. We would rise early. He, so that he could begin his duties; I, so that I would be there for the drawing of the lots. They did it twice a day, every day, morning and night.

Eleazar would gather with the other priests in his division by the entrance to the Holy Place, and I would mount the step to the top of the wall that divided the court of the priests from the court of the women. Often, especially at the drawing of the morning lots, there were just the priests in the court of the priests. On the wall of the court of the women there were two of us: me and one other woman.

She seemed old to me, as much in her spirit as in her outward appearance – as though life had worn her down. I noticed that she gazed as ardently at the ceremony as I did, her lips moving as she prayed for its outcome.

The process was laborious. The priests in the division would be separated into two groups. Then the High Priest would delve into the breastplate on his Ephod and bring out either the Urim or the Thummim. Urim selected one group, Thummim the other. The winning group would be split into two again and the whole process would begin again. Over and over the lot was drawn until just two remained. The final draw identified which would go in and tend to the incense.

I felt quite expert by the last day of Eleazar's week of service. Thirteen times the groups had been split, and thirteen times Eleazar had not been selected.

This final morning was his last chance this time around. The old woman arrived just after me, and we focused our gaze on the process as we had done thirteen times before. In the end, my curiosity got the better of me.

'Why do you want it to be him so much?' I asked, pointing at an elderly priest in the crowd below us. 'Surely he's tended the incense so many times before?'

The woman turned her gaze on me.

'No,' she said, her gentle eyes creasing as she smiled sadly. 'The lot has not fallen on Zechariah yet. Thirty years a priest and never chosen.' She sighed. 'I used to think we were God's favoured couple. How wrong I was. Him never chosen in the Temple – and me never chosen for a child.'

She patted her stomach wistfully. 'I asked him, when he was chosen, if he would pray for me … for us … for a child. I thought that if he prayed right next to the Holy of Holies, he could maybe whisper it right into God's ear. But he was never chosen … and neither was I. Now it's too late. I don't know why I keep on coming to the drawing of the lots. It's habit, I suppose.'

We turned back to the scene below us. Our conversation had absorbed us both so much that we hadn't noticed that the drawing of lots had reached the final two – Eleazar on one side and Zechariah on the other. I reached out and gripped Elizabeth's hand. All of a sudden, I was no longer as sure that I wanted the lot to fall on Eleazar.

We watched from our vantage point as the High Priest

dipped his hand one last time into the holy breastplate and pulled out a stone. He looked at it for a moment and then tipped his head towards Zechariah. Elizabeth exhaled loudly beside me.

'At last,' I heard her whisper. 'But it is too late.'

Zechariah glanced up at her, the wry look on his face indicating that he was thinking the same thing. Eleazar disappeared round the side of the Holy Place and reappeared a few moments later with an elaborate box, which he handed to Zechariah. The box contained the coals and incense for the Holy Place. Zechariah took it, gave one last, lingeringly thoughtful glance in the direction of Elizabeth, and entered the Holy Place.

USUALLY AFTER THE DRAWING OF LOTS I would descend once more into the court of the women and work my way slowly back to our temporary lodgings. But today I found I couldn't move. Today I felt I had to stay. So Elizabeth and I stood there, our hands clasped together … waiting. I had no idea what we were waiting for, but I did know that it was important to wait.

To begin with, everything seemed normal. The rituals associated with tending the incense were precise but brief. After the first while, when Zechariah didn't emerge again from the Holy Place, Elizabeth and I smiled at each other. He was making the most of it. Perhaps he was whispering their hearts' desire at the Temple veil after all, even though there was no point now.

The time ticked on but there was still no sign of him. At one point, I thought there was a faint glimmer around the Temple as though a bright light were shining inside but I shook my head: the excitement had made me fanciful.

The whole assembly gathered around the door, as was the custom, were getting restless. What should they do? It wasn't permitted to enter the Holy Place unless it was by lot to tend the space. I saw the High Priest step forward and turn in conversation to other senior-looking priests around him. Although I couldn't hear the words, their conversation was animated and involved much gesticulating. The High Priest threw up his hands in frustration but did nothing more. There was nothing they could do but wait.

What if he'd died in there?

I opened my mouth to ask but, glancing at Elizabeth's drawn face, promptly closed it again. She was the last person to ask. My thoughts gathered speed. Priests couldn't touch dead bodies. What would they do? What would happen to the Holy Place? Would death that close to the Holy of Holies render it unclean?

My thoughts spun onwards.

EVENTUALLY, THOUGH, WHEN WE'D all begun to give up hope, the door opened again, and Zechariah emerged. He looked as though he had aged about ten years in the time he had been inside, but strangely his face shone.

A hubbub broke out below me. Fragments of questions could be heard hanging in the air.

'What were you doing?'

'Why did it take so long?'

'What happened in there?'

Eventually the sounds died down and I saw the High Priest turn to Zechariah and say, 'Well?'

Silence fell on the gathering. A silence that stretched on and on. I saw Zechariah open his mouth, but no sound came out. He tried again but still there was nothing.

'He's spoken with God,' I heard Elizabeth whisper beside me. She turned to me, her eyes shining.

'At last, God has shown us favour.'

I watched her begin her descent back to the court of the women, but couldn't shake the feeling that God's favour wasn't quite what I used to think it was. It looked to me as though God's favour – when it came – turned your life inside out and upside down.

The Fourth Sunday of Advent
(Mary)
MARY'S STORY

The fourth Advent candle reminds us of Mary.

M Y NAME IS MIRIAM. You probably know me by another name – Mary. I think most people do these days.

I heard that name for the first time when I was a child. We lived in Sepphoris back then. It was a big bustling town, not like Nazareth where we live now. Nazareth is sleepy and out of the way. In Nazareth everyone knows everyone else … and everyone else's business, too. Sepphoris was different: large and wealthy and full of people from all over the world. When I was very little, I didn't know that. All the people I knew were Jewish like us. They all spoke Aramaic like we did. The people I knew, knew me, and called me by my name. Miriam.

My father was a potter and made storage jars to sell in the marketplace. They were the best storage jars in the whole of Galilee, and people would come from miles around to buy them. I used to beg to be allowed to go with him to the marketplace, but I was always too young. Then one day I was no longer too young, and I rode with him into town on his cart. It was a glorious day. I worked hard, fetching and carrying and smiling my joy at all his customers.

At the end of the day, I noticed an old Roman soldier sitting near our stall in the marketplace, basking in the late afternoon sun. He saw me looking at him and called me over.

'What's your name?' he asked.

'Miriam,' I told him.

'Maria,' he said back to me. 'A pretty name for a pretty child.'

I could see he was being kind, but he puzzled me. Maria wasn't my name, and pretty wasn't a word I'd ever thought of for myself. I said all of this to my father as we packed up the stall. Father had explained to me that the soldier was just saying my name in another language – his heart language – one I didn't know.

'Why doesn't he speak our language?' I objected. 'Everyone knows Aramaic.'

'Not everyone,' he'd said. 'And maybe he wants to be reminded of home.'

'But I'm clever and strong and quick,' I'd said, not yet ready to let my outrage go. 'I'm not pretty. I want him to think that I'm strong.'

My father had thrown back his head, then, and laughed. 'You have strong spirit, that's for sure.'

He turned and looked at me. 'Miriam,' he said, 'people will think of you whatever they choose. There's nothing you can do to control that. What you can do is find out who God created you to be. Live that life – and leave them to make of it what they will.'

I had grumbled at that. I didn't want people I didn't know changing my name and thinking whatever they felt like about me.

Tonight, as I sank wearily to the floor in the small, abandoned hut that Joseph had found for us on the way to Bethlehem, I remembered that day and the words of my father. I chuckled quietly to myself as Joseph bathed my poor swollen, tired feet.

'Did I tickle?' he asked solicitously.

'No,' I said, 'I was just remembering how, as a child, I wanted to protect myself against what other people thought about me. It seems rather futile now. People have thought so many things about me … about us … over the past few months. The thought I might have any control over it made me chuckle.'

Joseph paused, leaned over, and took my hand. 'It has been quite a time, hasn't it? The other day, I heard two people talking. One said that I knew the child was mine but was pretending it wasn't because I wanted to appear to be righteous. The other shouted over him and said it was clear you had lain with a Roman solider and were too afraid to admit it. They were so angry with each other they nearly came to blows – just as well they didn't notice me behind them.'

I sighed. 'If only that was the worst they'd said about us. Did you ever think of walking away, from me, from this, from it all?'

'Of course I did. You know that.'

'After the angel, I mean?'

Joseph smiled in that way of his, that meant the corners of his eyes wrinkled. 'Definitely not. It isn't every day an angel tells you what to do.'

'But you didn't choose this.'

'Neither did you.'

'No. But I did say yes.' I thought back to the moment that had changed my life so completely.

THE DAY HAD BEGUN LIKE any other day. The rest of the household was out, going about their usual business. I was at home in the cool, permanent twilight of our house, half-carved into the rock of the hillside. I was idly sweeping the floor. It always felt like a pointless task: dust settled almost as a fast as I could sweep it. Just then, the entire space was filled with light. I jumped in fright.

'Rejoice, favoured one,' the being had said.

I'd looked around wondering if there was someone behind me that this 'thing' full of light was speaking to but no one else was there. A thousand questions filled my mind. Who was this? Why had they come? Were they an angel? I'd never seen one before so couldn't be sure. Maybe they were? I wondered how you were meant to address an angel.

'Don't be afraid, Mary,' the what-I-presumed-to-be-an-angel had said. I was tempted to say that if he didn't want people to be afraid, he shouldn't arrive unannounced in their houses, knowing their names and scaring them witless. And then he'd told me that I was going to bear a son. I would call him 'Jesus,' he said. Jesus was going to be great and rule like David.

It made no sense. How could I be about to have a baby? I was a young girl, not even married yet. When I had been betrothed to Joseph my mother had sat me down and explained to me what was expected of a married woman. But the life she'd described was still before me. Despite what everyone now supposes, at that point I had barely met Joseph and had not even begun to imagine my future life. So I struggled to understand what the angel might mean. A baby? Me? How could that be?

The angel tried to explain but my brain took nothing more in. At the end the angel added (almost as an afterthought it seemed), 'Nothing will be impossible with God.'

In that moment something shifted in me.

Nothing will be impossible with God.' Suddenly, I was filled with clarity. I knew he was right. Nothing would be impossible. Lots of things would be difficult – but nothing would be impossible. My mouth moved and I heard a voice that sounded like my own agreeing to it. All of it. Unimaginable though it was.

I LOOKED AT JOSEPH AND REPEATED, 'I did say yes.'

'And so did I,' he said.

Joseph had told me at the time about the angel who had appeared while he was sleeping. He had come round almost before it was light the next day and we'd held the simplest of ceremonies before he'd taken me back to his house. He'd hoped that it would save me from the worst of the gossip, but the word had already got out. The whispers of scandal spreading more quickly than even the biting winter wind currently whipping through this abandoned hut could blow.

'What will become of us?' I asked him wearily. 'I don't even understand why we have to go to Bethlehem at all.'

'No, I don't either,' he said. 'I'd heard nothing of a census until Cousin Simeon announced it last week as he passed through, but it seems most sensible to go just in case. Besides, I imagine a break from the gossip might do you good.'

It would, of course, but I was tired and disheartened, and we still had a long way to go. At that moment, the baby stretched, a foot poking its way outwards just under my rib cage. I pushed it back in again, but as I did a flood of warmth filled my heart.

'Nothing will be impossible with God,' I whispered, and the baby fluttered a little as though in agreement with me.

'I wonder what they'll say about him,' I mused. 'After he's born. Will they understand him more than they understand us?'

'It's unlikely,' Joseph answered. 'After all, I'm not sure I do.'

I had to nod my agreement at that. There were moments when I felt I could almost glimpse the edges of what it all meant: when the angel had explained it first in my home; when I saw Cousin Elizabeth in the hill country and a song had burst out of me fully formed. But at other times the picture faded again.

This was a special baby, I knew that. He'd caused enough trouble already for me to know that he was special. But who would he be? Would I understand him? Would anyone else?

I PLACED A HAND ON MY STOMACH and Joseph placed his on top of mine. It felt – or maybe I imagined it – that the baby pressed up against our hands. 'Nothing will be impossible with God,' we said again.

'Now all we have to do is believe it to be true,' said Joseph.

'And get to Bethlehem,' I added.

'Once we get there, everything will be normal and straightforward,' he said reassuringly.

The baby trembled beneath my hand. If I didn't know better, I'd have thought he was laughing.

SHIPHRAH'S STORY

M Y NAME IS SHIPHRAH. Well, it isn't *really*, but it is what everyone calls me.

My real name is Dinah, but, years ago, after a young neighbour had a difficult birth, I had battled for hours to save the life of a mother and her baby. Afterwards someone quipped that I was their very own 'Shiphrah.' I threw up my hands at that, protesting that Shiphrah and Puah had risked their lives to save the lives of countless Hebrew boys in Egypt; all I'd done was use my skill to save two lives.

Secretly, though, a warm glow spread through me: I was pleased by the comparison with my ancestor in life and faith, and even more delighted when the name caught on. 'Call for Shiphrah,' people say when a woman's time is near and I go running, no matter what the time, day or night.

There is no finer feeling in all the world than to be the one ready to greet a new life as they enter the world: praying God's blessing on them and then handing them into the care of their mothers.

Right now, however, I am relieved that there are no babies due in Bethlehem: Rebekah's baby came last month, and Esther's isn't due for a while yet. So my skills won't be needed. It's just as well, because our house is bursting at the seams.

WE LIVE IN BETHLEHEM, my husband Saul and I. We have one of the biggest houses in the town. Not as large as some of the houses in Jerusalem but big, nevertheless.

Lots of room upstairs for our family, with room to spare for any passing guests and a separate area downstairs for the animals.

Normally the house feels spacious and airy, but over the past few weeks people have started arriving at our door. My husband's second cousin, then my nephew and his wife. After them, friends of friends until the house is fuller than I have ever known it. My serving girl Naomi and I are busy dawn till dusk, hurrying here and there, fetching and carrying, making sure all our many guests are cared for.

'What have they all come for?' I wailed to Saul. Of course, I was pleased to welcome them. My mother had taught me the gift and importance of hospitality. No friends or stranger seeking refuge would ever be turned from my door. But this was getting ridiculous.

'I'm not really sure,' he shrugged. 'There's a rumour about a census, so everyone is travelling to their ancestral home, just in case.'

'Just in case of what?'

'Well, you never know with the Romans, it's always better to look like you're doing what they say.'

I tutted. 'The Romans.' We talked about them all the time. They filled our lives with dread, often more by what we imagined they would do than what we had seen with our own eyes. The fear of them was what kept us subdued. I sensed it everywhere I went – the horror of what they might do hanging over us, never leaving us.

This latest product of that fear was a house full of guests – and full of noise. Everywhere I looked, someone was there, taking up space and making their needs known. I tried to remind myself that I was delighted to look after them, but even I wasn't convinced by my attempt.

THEN, ONE DAY, EARLY in the morning I heard a weary knock at the street door. My frustration bubbled over and I yelled more loudly than I meant to that we couldn't welcome anyone else and that there really was no more room – unless they didn't mind sleeping with the animals.

My husband went to open the door, with me a few steps behind him. I opened my mouth ready to say that enough was enough and we were sorry, but they would have to look elsewhere. But then I checked myself: this was no stranger.

'Cousin Joseph?' I said, hesitantly. His father had moved north years ago, but we had played together as children, and I had never forgotten him.

He smiled, his tired face breaking into a familiar warm grin. So much about him had changed since I saw him last, but I'd recognize that smile anywhere.

'You have a full house,' he observed. I flushed with embarrassment. (Clearly my voice had carried as far as street outside.) 'It took us longer to get here than I thought it would.'

'You heard the census rumour too?' My husband asked.

'Yes,' Joseph replied. 'It looks like everyone else had the same idea as us: travel home just in case we need to be here. But Mary's progress was slower than usual.'

He moved slightly so I could see the person beside him, leaning her full weight on his arm. She was a young woman, little more than a girl really. She was heavily pregnant and breathing shallowly in the way women do when the baby they carry has grown so large that there is no room left for a full breath. She appeared to be at the very end of her strength. Drops of sweat stood out on her forehead and her face twisted momentarily in pain.

'It looks as though you got here just in time,' my husband said. 'We'll move some of our guests out of the upper room.'

'Where to?' My irritation spilled over once more.

Mary, standing at the door, moaned gently and gripped Joseph's arm so tightly that he winced. My frustrations melted away in a single moment, as years of experience drew my full attention onto the woman in front of me. Her baby was on its way.

'We're too late for that,' I said. 'I don't think Mary could get up those stairs now.'

She shook her head gratefully. She glanced at Joseph, who seemed torn between his concern for her and terror at what was to come.

'Don't worry,' Saul said to him, 'Shiphrah will take care of Mary. Come with me.' Joseph slumped with relief as Saul put his arm around him and guided him up the stairs to the overfull living space.

'You weren't joking about the animals,' Mary said in a gap between her labour pains, as I settled her into the straw next to the feeding trough.

'Quietest and safest place for you right now,' I reassured her.

The hours passed slowly, as they always did during labour. Waves of anguish wracked Mary, as the instincts of her young body took over and pushed the baby into the world.

Not for the first time, I reflected that there was a reason this was called labour. No labourer worked harder than a woman when she gave birth. As time went on, Mary became increasingly exhausted. I looked at her anxiously from below my lashes. The long journey from Nazareth followed by a difficult labouring had used up more of her strength than I was comfortable with. Over the years, I had seen far too many women lose their own lives even as they wrestled to bring new life into the world.

'Perhaps someday the Lord God himself should be made to be born as a baby,' I said at one point, through gritted teeth. 'Then he might find a better way to bring new life into the world.'

Mary looked at me and seemed about to say something, but another wave of agony overtook her, and her words were swallowed in a scream of pain.

At long last, when the night sky outside the house was

at its darkest, Mary's baby was born. A healthy baby boy, who announced his arrival into the world with a lusty cry. The sounds of rejoicing from above us in the house indicated that our houseful of guests had laboured with us in spirit through the long pain-filled hours.

I held his tiny form wonderingly in my wrinkled, coarse hands. This was the moment that made all that labouring worthwhile. Here was a baby, like hundreds of babies before him, who was taking his first tentative breaths in this strange and dangerous world. He screwed up his eyes and wailed piercingly. I looked up at Mary, whose face was shining with weary delight, and back again to the baby. He took a breath, ready for another cry, but then paused. His large, dark eyes opened, and it felt as though he was looking right at me and that his gaze shone with a wisdom that reached back to the very dawn of time.

I hesitated. This was a moment I had experienced so many times before – and yet had never felt like this. This time, it felt as though I held in my arms not just a new life but life itself. This time, it felt as though I was looking hope in the eye. I shook my head. I was getting fanciful in my old age.

I swaddled him deftly and laid him in the feeding trough. It was the safest place for him. A baby as small as this would risk being trampled in the living quarters above. I turned as Joseph reached the bottom of the steps, his face beaming with joy.

'I put little Joseph in the feeding trough,' I told him.

He smiled, 'Not Joseph. His name is Jesus – Saviour.

He has come to save God's people.'

I laughed. Parents always had bold notions for their children but this was beyond anything I had ever heard before.

'You'll see,' said Joseph.

All of a sudden, I needed a moment alone. Something was different. Something important had changed and I couldn't work out what it was. I stepped out into the street and looked back through the window at the new family. Joseph's grandiose words were still ringing in my ears. How ridiculous that he should say such a thing! A baby as important as that wouldn't be left to be born like this.

I FELT A PRESENCE AT MY SIDE and looked down to see Naomi, who had followed me out with a new swaddling cloth for when the baby soiled the first one.

'What's that light?' she asked.

I looked up. She was right: the night sky had an odd sheen as though something had recently been shining in it.

Just then, a noise at the end of the street made us both turn. There, hurrying in my direction was a group of shepherds, laughing and chattering with excitement. What on earth were they doing here at this time of night? Surely they hadn't left their sheep alone on the hillside? They were heading right for us.

I readied myself. If they thought they were coming into my house, they could think again.

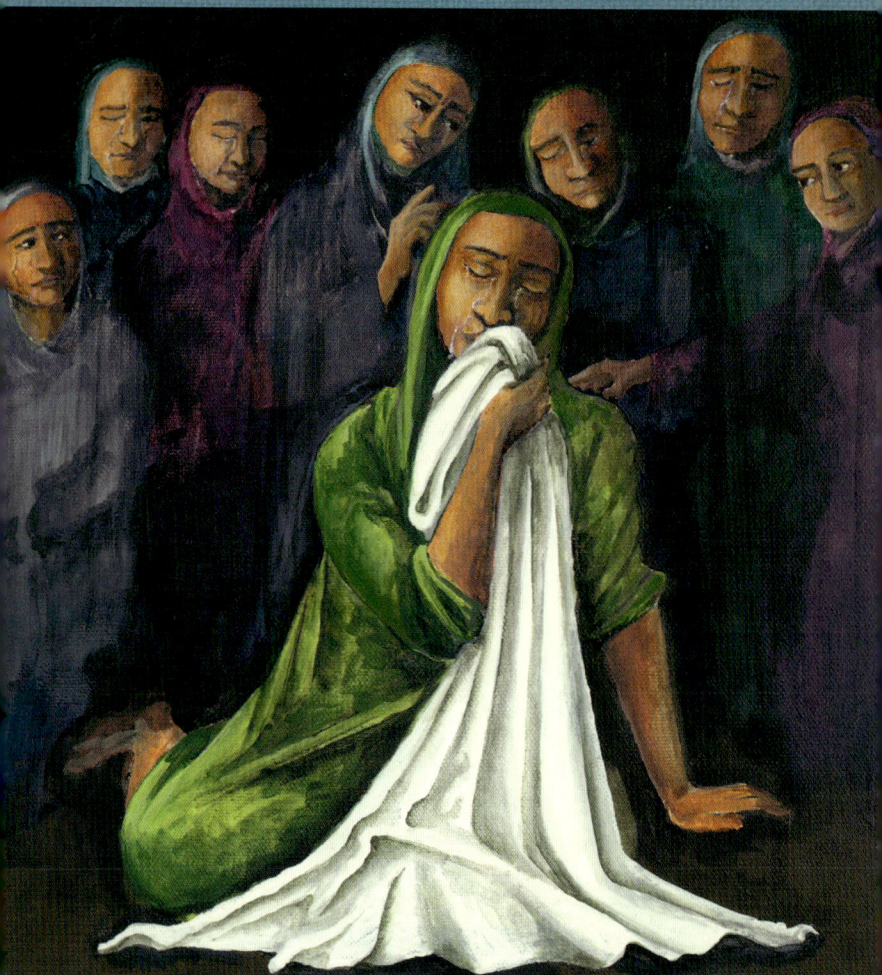

The Holy Innocents
(28 December)

RACHEL'S STORY

Rachel's Story and Mariamne's Story (p. 59) are the wrong way round if you follow Matthew's Gospel, where the visit of the wise men comes before Herod's slaughter of the innocents. But the Western Church calendar marks Holy Innocents on 28 December, ahead of the Epiphany (6 January). You might prefer to read the stories in a different order.

M Y NAME IS RACHEL. I've lived in Bethlehem all my life. First with my family, and now (a few houses away) with my husband's family.

My father owns sheep. Before I married, I would join my brother on the hills around Bethlehem watching over the sheep, making sure they came to no harm. I look back on those days now and wish I could run away, run back through the years to that simpler time.

Then we would sit on the hillside for hours, watching over the sheep. The years have washed away the challenges of that life, so that now as I look back the sun's rays were always warm but never overpowering, the breeze refreshing but never cold, the sheep contented and full, never straying and never wracked with hunger.

There would be no sound other than that of the other boys (who, of course, in my memory never bickered and fought), practising the sling shot for when the wild animals came, or singing psalms to the sound of my brother's lyre. My parents had called him David after our great king and ancestor, and, as the shepherds and I would joke, it had quite gone to his head. If Goliath had happened by, we reckoned our David would have had a go at felling him. David would smile, and incline his head slightly, his shining eyes indicating that this was no joke at all and in his mind's eye he was already holding the giant's head aloft in victory.

I was named after an ancestor too: Rachel, Jacob's beloved wife, mother of Joseph and Benjamin. When the sun beat down in the summer and the grass dried up, we would range further with the sheep and sometimes we would go to the place my brother David said was Rachel's tomb, just north of our town. Sometimes when we were sitting on the hillside at night, the wind would blow from that direction, and you would hear a strange wailing sound all around.

'It's Rachel,' David would say dramatically, 'weeping for her children. She refuses to be comforted because they are no more.'

'Don't be ridiculous.' This would be Amos, who is now my husband. 'It's just the wind hitting Rachel's tomb from a particular direction.' Like his namesake, Amos felt the need to tell the truth at all times, no matter how unpopular that made him.

For years, these memories had filled me with a warm glow. The nostalgia had carried me through the strangeness of a new marriage, the drudgery of housework, the terror of childbirth and the responsibility of new motherhood. When life felt too much, I drifted back to a simpler time, when I had been a shepherd girl on the hillside. Of course,

I had edited out the cold and discomfort, the sorrow when, despite our best efforts, a wild animal had carried off a lamb; and the endless fighting between the other shepherds who knew how to annoy each other with unerring precision.

So tonight, as I sit outside my house in the middle of the street with my neighbours gathered around me, waiting – all of us hoping against hope that what we fear most has not happened – I find myself back there again on the hillside: the gentle summer sun warming my back, the sheep baa-ing gently around me, David sitting a little way off, singing about the Lord who is his shepherd.

It's years since I have been out on the hillside in person.

My life is now taken up with a husband and a beautiful baby boy who is very nearly two, as well as a house to take care of.

My father died a few years ago, and now David takes care of the sheep with Amos' help. Most of the time he no longer sits out on the hillside (that's a job for the young), but a while back he had been there, and so had Amos. They were shorthanded so had gone to watch over the sheep themselves.

Their story the next day was a jumble. They'd been watching quietly by the entrance to the sheep pen. A lion had been seen a few days before and they were worried it might come back for the sheep, so they had been particularly alert, they said.

Then suddenly there was a flash of light – and there was an angel right there in front of them. I asked them what the angel looked like, but they said they couldn't see, the light was too bright. The angel told them about a baby being born who was the Messiah. And then the whole sky had been filled with the heavenly host singing about glory to God and peace on earth.

It was the strangest story. I had to get them to tell it to me quite a few times, and even now after all this time I'm not sure what to believe. But David and Amos rarely agree on anything, and they do agree on this. So something must have happened.

They did apparently rush down to Bethlehem to see the baby, which had been born in the midwife's house. They had to beg Shiphrah to let them in, but David can be persuasive when he tries and, eventually, she relented and they saw him. They'd put him in a feeding trough to keep him safe, apparently. But it seems so unlikely. A Messiah? Born in this small town? Laid in a feeding trough?

Surely no one would believe that … would they?

IT TURNS OUT THAT SOMEBODY did believe it; and the very worst somebody at that.

Apparently, King Herod was told that a baby had been born to be the Messiah. My neighbours think it must have been those wealthy strangers that passed through a week or so ago. They were the talk of the town in their outlandish clothing, wafting exotic smells and trailing vast numbers of servants. They had visited Shiphrah's house, just like David and Amos and the other shepherds had done. And then they were gone. Soon after, so were the couple and their baby, apparently. They had slipped away in the dead of night without anyone seeing them.

We told Herod's soldiers this when they came. Over and over again we screamed at them that the baby wasn't here anymore, but they didn't listen. They rampaged through the town, pulling babies out of their mothers' arms as they went. Our house was the last in the town, the last one they came to. When I had seen them coming – when I had realized what they were there to do – I had run home with my baby and hid, hoping they might pass me by. But he was restless and frightened and, hard as I tried to quieten him, he wouldn't stop crying.

The soldiers heard him and took him. I wouldn't let him go, so they pulled me out into the street with him, striking me with the hilt of their swords over and over again to make me let him go. Eventually I couldn't hold on anymore and they wrenched him from my arms.

My brother and husband had followed them then. I don't know what they thought they could do but they clearly felt the need to do something. I heard their angry, terrified voices fading away into the distance as they pursued the soldiers out of the town.

Then there was silence.

I HELD ONTO THE ONLY THING I had left of my boy, his swaddling cloth that was still warm from the heat of his small body. And we waited. It felt as though all the women who had ever lived in this place waited with us.

Silence filled the town.

At last our men came back, limping and bruised, bleeding and shuffling in their defeat.

They had fought for our babies, every last one of them, but Herod's soldiers were too strong, too intent on their horrific task.

David and Amos reached me at the same time, blood pouring from their many wounds, the horror of what they had witnessed written all over their faces.

At that moment the wind shifted, and the sound of the wind reached us from Rachel's tomb, its unearthly, keening tone barely heard above the wailing of our own voices.

'Listen,' said David, 'A voice was heard in Ramah, wailing and loud lamentation.'

I looked at Amos, half expecting him to disagree with David as he had done so many times in our childhood. But he didn't. He reached out his hand instead and continued, his voice breaking as he spoke.

'Rachel is weeping for her children. She refuses to be comforted because they are no more.'

I lifted my head, our boy's swaddling cloth still clutched in my hand, the words catching in my throat.

'Rachel weeps with us and will never stop. Pray God there comes a time in our land when her weeping can cease.'

In the distance, the eerie sound continued, and we wept along with it, a haunting accompaniment to our grief.

The Naming and Circumcision of Jesus
(1 January)

ELIZABETH'S STORY

The First Sunday of Advent
(The Patriarchs)

SARAH'S STORY

THE
STORIES

MY NAME IS ELIZABETH. I live, with my husband Zechariah, in En Kerem, alongside many other priestly families, ready and poised for the next time they will serve in the Temple in Jerusalem.

Ours are noble families, his and mine. He can trace his line back to Abijah, grandson of Aaron. Mine goes back even further – to Aaron himself.

But it's best not to mention that too often. It never goes down very well.

WHEN WE FIRST MARRIED we were a golden couple, Zechariah and I: our two ancient families united in marriage, honoured and envied by all our neighbours. I would hear their voices whispering as we passed, as they retold our family histories to each other with awe.

Slowly, bit by bit, the whispering changed. When, after a few months, there was no sign of a child, eyebrows were raised, questions whispered behind hands.

Then, as months turned into years, people started glancing in my direction as though I was in some way tarnished. They pulled away when I approached, as though whatever was wrong with me might be catching. Conversations that used to include me faltered at my approach. It was as though they thought that if they didn't say the words in my presence, I wouldn't know what they had been talking about. They seemed to be unaware that the air was still crackling with their suddenly halted gossip. As though those awful words – 'barren', 'dried up', 'worthless', 'cursed by God' – weren't still hanging above their heads. After a while even that stopped. After twenty years even the scandal of Jericho's golden couple being childless stopped being newsworthy.

I coped well with the gossip on the outside, my chin held high, my eyes challenging anyone to say it to my face, which of course they never did. At home, however, I would sob out my sorrow and loneliness, asking over and over again why God didn't favour me. Why? And Zechariah would pat my arm helplessly. He had no answers either.

Despite it all, ours was a good life most of the time. The great gift of having a number of priests crammed together in one space is that it gives them ample opportunity to air their views on what is right and what is not. The problem is they rarely agree. Many a night's sleep is disturbed by the sound of disagreements raging in the street outside – as ideas are put forward, knocked down and debated repeatedly. There is nothing so delectable to my neighbours as a good meaty argument. But there is one thing upon which everyone agrees: the importance of tradition. Doing things as they have always been done, time immemorial. That's what priests are for: knowing the tradition, keeping the tradition, and handing it on pristine to the next generation.

And there is no tradition more worthy of upholding than the tradition of family. Passing down names and history and memories from one generation to another. It is, after all, how I know my family can be traced to Aaron, whereas Zechariah's only goes back to Abijah.

So I knew it would cause trouble as soon as Zechariah told me. Though he didn't so much tell me as write it down.

He had to after all.

WHEN WE CAME BACK FROM the Temple on that memorable day, Zechariah couldn't say a word.

He would open and close his mouth passionately, but not a single sound emerged. He gestured, and waved his arms around and wrote a few things down. Slowly, I pieced it all together.

Right there in the Holy of Holies, he'd seen an angel. I know it sounds mad, doesn't it?

He had seen an angel and the angel had taken his voice away. But that wasn't the weirdest thing he had to communicate. Far stranger than the angel who took his voice away was that the angel said I would bear a child.

I'd followed Zechariah's tall tale with a straight face until then, but that did it. I laughed so much I had to sit down. I laughed until tears started rolling down my cheeks – at least that was what I told him – my laughter was too close to crying for comfort. The dear old thing. All that praying had addled his brain. An angel announcing that a dried old stick like me would bear a child? Whatever next? The poor old man, he wasn't right in his head.

I hid Zechariah away then. I didn't want people pointing and laughing at his poor, befuddled, silent self.

But eventually I had to take it back. Not right away, you understand, but after a while.

When the morning sickness came day after day, and my stomach began to swell. In the end I was hiding myself away, not him. It turned out that I didn't want them pointing and laughing at me. So, none of our neighbours really knew what had happened back there in the Temple. Zechariah couldn't tell them – and I didn't want to.

Imagine their shock, then, when our son was born and they went to circumcise him and name him Zechariah – after his father and his father's father and his father's father's father.

Imagine their shock when I said, 'No. His name is John.'

Full of consternation and horror, they turned to Zechariah, who wrote it down so they could all see.

His name is John.

ALL OF THAT HAPPENED a few months ago now. And, like before, I steeled myself for the gossip.

I'd see people on street corners waving their arms and gesticulating their outrage and then falling silent as a I passed by. But this time I cared much less. I had my heart's desire. My John, whom I held to my heart and loved and loved.

He wasn't an easy baby. Even from the first day, he had such a mind of his own.

'Contrary,' the neighbours remarked, disapprovingly.

'That's what happens,' they said, 'when you break with tradition: nothing is ever goes right.'

'What kind of man would a child like that grow up to be?' they said. 'He could cause all kinds of trouble.'

But I got on with our new life, and slowly the gossip died down. Until today, that is. Today it all began again.

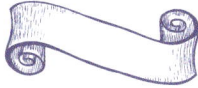

THERE THEY WERE AGAIN, casting significant glances in my direction, waving their arms around, pursing their lips with disapproval.

Eventually I heard what I had happened. Zechariah (whose voice had returned in full by now) told me, a gentle twinkle in his eye.

My young cousin, Mary – the one who had come to stay while John was in the womb. Her baby had been born.

There were wild tales, Zechariah said, of hosts of angels filling the sky with their singing.

'There was me,' he said, 'with only one angel. And you thought that was wild enough.'

I had to grin and admit that I had.

'So, is that what they're talking about?' I asked him.

He put his head back and roared with laughter.

'No,' he said. 'Even a whole sky full of angels isn't enough to distract them from the outrage. What they're talking about is his name.'

'Joseph?' I asked. Though, as I asked, I knew what he'd say.

'No,' he answered. 'They called him Jesus.'

Two small names – John (the Lord is Gracious) and Jesus (the Lord is salvation). Two small names and two small babies.

I held John close to my heart and rocked him. He squirmed in my grip and looked at me fiercely.

'These two little ones are causing a stir before they've even had time to do anything,' I said, a sense of foreboding creeping over me. 'Let's hope that their names will be the most revolutionary thing about them.'

'I think that is unlikely,' Zechariah said gently. 'These two, between them, are going to turn the world on its head, and I'm not sure the world will like it.'

He turned at the door, a thoughtful look on his face.

'We used to wish that God would favour us,' he said. 'Our wish has come true. But I fear – as so often with God's favour – that we might have got more than we bargained for.'

MARIAMNE'S STORY

Y NAME IS MARIAMNE. Though what most people call me these days is 'the second Mariamne', or 'the other Mariamne'. Unless, of course, they are a Hasmonean and related to the first Mariamne. What they call me is much less flattering and probably best not mentioned.

My husband Herod is still mad with grief even now, over twenty years after the death of the original Mariamne. When I say 'death', I should probably say 'execution'. And when I say 'execution', I should add 'at the instigation of Herod'.

I know this sounds far-fetched, but that isn't the worst of it. Herod's court is made up of a web of madness that holds everything and everyone in its thrall. But you can get used to anything after a while.

You only realize how mad it sounds when you explain it to a stranger.

I'VE JUST DONE THAT. I explained everything to some strangers who were passing through and watched as their eyes grew bigger and bigger.

They were magi from the East. The whole court was buzzing with stories of their riches and their wisdom, their exotic tales and their questions. They had come, they said, because they'd seen the rising of a new star. We hung on their every word. They told us how they watched the stars and saw how they changed. They explained how they worked out what the stars were telling them. They rolled out their charts and their holy books and showed us what they revealed.

Their passion was infectious. Everyone they met was desperate to know the meaning of this momentous new star. A new beginning had come. Who could not be enthralled by the prospect?

To begin with, Herod was as enchanted as the rest of us. And then it all went wrong. The magi turned to Herod, their eyes shining and asked:

'Where is the child who has been born King of the Jews?'

A deathly silence fell over the court. We gazed fixedly at the floor.

The magi appeared not to notice and continued blithely onwards. 'The new star marked his birth, we have come to worship him.'

Herod, who had turned an alarming purply red colour, turned on his heel and left.

You could hear Herod's rage echoing through the corridors, calling for the chief priests and the scribes, for anyone in fact who might tell him what was going on. As I left the throne room, I couldn't help noticing how quiet the palace was. News had got out fast and people were fleeing lest the wrath of Herod fell on them.

I summoned the magi later that day.

'But majesty,' implored the head steward, 'what if the King finds out?'

'You'd better make sure he doesn't,' I said, my voice sounding more confident than I felt.

So I told them everything.

How Herod had gained the confidence of the Romans over many years until they made him King. How he knew – and the rest of Galilee and Judea knew – that he had no right to be king. How he feared a usurper around every corner. How he had killed countless members of his own family who he feared would rival him as king. How he even had his most beloved wife – the first Mariamne – executed because he feared she would overthrow him. How he had heard of me and married me to replace his lost first love. How he was tormented with fear every moment of every day. How his murderous anger would spill over at the slightest provocation.

The magi sat and listened, their eyes (which became bigger and bigger as I spoke) the only sign that they were taking in the enormity of what I was saying.

'What will you do? I asked them at the end.

'The gods will guide us,' one of them replied.

The others nodded and I felt a rush of envy. These men took their guidance from above, not from the capricious court of Herod in which one day you were Queen, and the next, a dead body, executed by a jealous King.

They had a solidity and peace that came from years of study, reflection and prayer.

'Maybe *your* God will guide us,' another of them added.

At that moment a servant came and whispered quietly in their ears. They bowed low and backed out of the room, as courtiers from the East often did.

Before they left, the one who had spoken last paused.

'The Messiah we seek has come to save you, too,' he said.

'It's too late for me,' I mumbled.

It felt that way. There was no saving for me. It felt as though I was caught in a dark web of something I didn't understand and in which I had no power to do anything. I was, after all, only the second Mariamne. An extra wife brought in to assuage the grief of man who, in the grip of fear, had killed my predecessor. The arrival of these strangers had reignited that fear again. Who knew where the focus of his terror would fall next? This could well be my last day in this life.

But the magus had continued to speak.

'There is more to this world that what the eye can see and the ear can hear. Your prophets know this, too,' he said. 'Listen to them. When you glimpse the things of heaven, the only thing to do is to fall to your knees in awe and wonder. When you catch sight of the things of heaven, you see the things of earth for what they really are. Don't be held captive by what is driven by fear – turn your heart to the source of all love.'

I opened my mouth to ask him what he meant. What difference would that make? Herod could well kill me anyway.

But he had already gone.

I didn't understand what he meant, but I did know that he was being kind and that was a balm to my troubled soul.

I WENT UP TO THE ROOF of the palace. It had always been my favourite place. I would look out over the roofs of the city and imagine myself to be a bird flying far away from the turmoil and despair of the court.

Everyone I met told me how lucky I was. The problem was, I didn't feel lucky; I felt trapped.

I had never wanted to be Queen. My father was a simple priest from Alexandria, with few ambitions until Herod came along. We lived a simple (and I now realize, happy) life, first in Alexandria and then in Jerusalem.

People say I am beautiful. I don't really know what that means, but everyone else seems to. The word of my beauty spread and spread until Herod heard of it. Apparently, he was captivated by tales of me, even more so when he heard of my name. I could replace his long-lost love, he told me when at last I met him. I couldn't help wondering if I would take Mariamne's place in death, too.

Herod was unstoppable. He couldn't marry a commoner like me, so he made sure I was no longer common, deposing the High Priest and replacing him with my father. Who could object to him marrying the daughter of a High Priest? Well, I could, but they never asked me. So, for twenty long years I had lived a life I didn't chose and didn't want, tossed this way and that by the ups and downs of court life.

Here on the roof, I felt freed from all that. In the palace I felt like a caged bird, kept until my owner grew bored of me – or worse. Here, I felt as though I could breathe.

FAR BELOW ME ON ANOTHER PART of the roof, the magi came out, clearly finished after their audience with Herod.

They had with them their maps and charts. They looked from them to the sky and back again. The sky was cloudy, and their vision was clearly obscured. They scratched their heads and looked back at their charts.

Just then a gap opened in the clouds and a single star shone through. It seemed brighter than any star I had ever seen. The magi clapped their hands with joy, rolled up the charts and maps and hurried off the roof.

The star shone down on me, and after a while I began to feel less alone, less afraid.

After a bit longer, I felt the stirring of something I had not felt since my youth. What was it? There was a warmth, a flicker of hope. I looked up at the star which shone and shone as though there was no darkness around it at all. I felt the urge, suddenly, to kneel, to bow down before something that was greater than me – greater than I could imagine.

Maybe the magus had been right after all? Maybe the Messiah had come to save me, too?

Above me the star twinkled brightly, as though its light was drawn from somewhere else, somewhere where there was no darkness at all.

ANNA'S STORY

Y NAME IS ANNA. I am a prophet. People say that I live on my own in the Temple. I don't. There's no such thing as being on your own in the Temple. People bustle past day and night. Priests on their way to their rituals; Levites tuning their instruments or bringing supplies for the incense burners; Rabbis with trails of disciples in their wake; earnest worshippers bringing their sacrifices to the altar. Even late at night, people pass backwards and forwards through the court of the women.

The Levites used to ask me why I had to sleep right here in the court of the women. Wouldn't I be more comfortable, they asked, in the court of the Gentiles, under the colonnades where the Rabbis teach and discuss all day? Or maybe in my own home where I wouldn't be in anyone's way?

They don't ask me that any more. After eighty-four years, they don't ask any more. I'm no less inconvenient to them, but after all this time they've got tired of asking.

So, no, I am not alone. But even if there was no one else in the Temple at all, there would be God.

EIGHTY-FOUR YEARS AGO NOW, the word of the Lord came to me.

Before then, I'd always wondered what it was like when God spoke. The prophets in the Scriptures mentioned God speaking to them as though we all know what that was like. 'The word of the Lord came to me,' they say. But

I'd always wanted to know what that was like. Did they see something, like Isaiah in the Temple? Or did they just hear something? A voice, maybe, whispering in their ear? Or was there a gossamer-thin silence, like Elijah reported on Mount Horeb?

'What do you think it feels like when the God speaks?' I'd ask my husband.

'I've never thought about it,' he would say.

'Wouldn't you like to think about?' I'd ask.

'Not really.'

I asked him a lot – because I thought about it a lot.

You see, I used to yearn for God to speak to me. Not just because I was curious (though I was), but because in the Scriptures, when an angel appeared or the word of Lord came, often a woman would conceive a child. This was something I longed for more than anything in the whole world.

'Aren't I enough for you?' my husband would ask, his gentle face creased with sorrow.

And I would shrug and shake my head, because I didn't want to hurt him by saying the words that we both know were true. I wasn't enough for him either, but he didn't feel the loss physically like I did. His body didn't mark his failure to conceive month in, month out, like mine did.

Then, he died.

We'd only been married for seven years. One morning a fever took hold of him, and by the evening he was dead. One moment he was there, and then he was gone.

The darkness of grief overtook me. And there is no

darker grief than grief laced with guilt. For seven long years I had grieved the lack of a child. It was only when he was gone – when it was too late – that I realized what I used to have and now had lost. Then the darkness wrapped around me as though it would never let me go.

IT WAS IN THE DARKNESS that the word of the Lord came to me.

When it came, I realized that my questions about what it was like when God spoke had been all wrong. When it came, the word of the Lord was nothing like anything else I'd ever experienced. It wasn't a vision. It wasn't a voice. It wasn't silence or a sound. It was like all of those things and none of them. It was a knowing that formed deep inside of me.

I didn't greet it, this 'knowing', as I should have done.

'Now you come,' I said in my bitterness. 'Now you come, when it is too late and all is lost.'

God settled down and waited while I vented all my sorrow and heartbreak and anger. At last, when I'd run out of energy, God reminded me that I was loved. But my heart was too wounded to receive this news, so I shouted again. And again I was reminded I was loved. On and on this went until, at last, love won. Not all at once, of course, but bit by bit.

'What do I do now?' I asked God, when I could speak again.

'You wait,' God replied. 'Love will come. Salvation will appear in a form you least expect.'

'How will I know it, when I see it?' I asked.

'You will,' God said.

And that was it. The word of the Lord came to me and didn't give me what my heart yearned for, nor returned what I had lost. God spoke and commanded me to wait. Somehow, over the years, I have learned that this is enough.

So, YOU SEE, I CAN'T WAIT in the court of the Gentiles under the colonnades, gracefully out of the way.

I must be as close to God as I can be. That's where I am, right next to the entrance to the Holy Place, in the place where people come to pay their Temple tax. I can't go closer. God could never a bear a woman's presence that close – or so the priests say. I stay as close as I'm allowed and I wait: fasting and praying, reading the Scriptures and hoping. From time to time, the word of the Lord – that deep knowing – comes to me and I tell those around me what it says. That's why they call me a prophet. But what they don't know is what I'm waiting for.

For eighty-four years I've waited. When I grow tired and think about giving up, the word of the Lord nudges me again and reminds me of love.

TODAY I WAS IN MY CORNER by the entrance to the Holy Place, when I noticed a couple with a tiny baby. They were wending their way through the crowds in the Temple to make a sacrifice with a pair of pigeons.

They'd just entered the court of the women when Simeon overtook them. He lives in Jerusalem and often stops to talk with me when he comes into the Temple. He arrived in a hurry, slightly breathless, as though he'd run all the way. Simeon took the baby in his arms unceremoniously. The couple – the baby's parents – shrugged as though they were quite used to strange things happening around their baby. I couldn't hear what Simeon was saying, but his face was suffused with joy as though he was declaring something momentous.

He gave the baby back and said something more to the woman, who blanched at his words. They continued towards the Holy Place more slowly now, as though troubled by whatever Simeon had said to them.

And then it happened. The word of the Lord came to me, and I knew – more clearly than I had ever known anything before in my life – that this was what I was waiting for. This was who I had waited for through eighty-four long years.

Here was love. Here was salvation. Here was the redemption of Israel.

'A baby?' I whispered to God.

'I told you it would come in a form you didn't expect.'

'Yes, but a baby – is that a good idea?'

'The very best.'

So I stumbled forward and took the baby clean out of his mother's arms. She sighed as though this baby had brought a lot of strangers unbidden into her life who had all acted as oddly as I was acting. Without thinking, the words of praise I heard sung around me every day came to my lips: *'O give thanks to the LORD, for he is good: his steadfast love endures for ever.'*

The child wriggled in my arms, opened his eyes and looked (or so it felt) right into my soul. And I knew that the love that had held me in the darkness when I needed it most was here now, cradled in my arms.

'This really wasn't what I was expecting,' I said to God.

'Thank you,' God replied. 'This is just the beginning. There's much more to come.'

'But will they know?' I asked, 'Will they know who he is?'

'Maybe you should tell them.'

So I did.

I told everyone that I could find – people who cared about the redemption of Jerusalem. I told them everything. And they smiled at me pityingly, as though I'd grown mad in my old age.

But I didn't care. I had held salvation in my arms. I had cradled eternal love and sung my own poor love song in return.

And I'd only had to wait eighty-four years to do so.

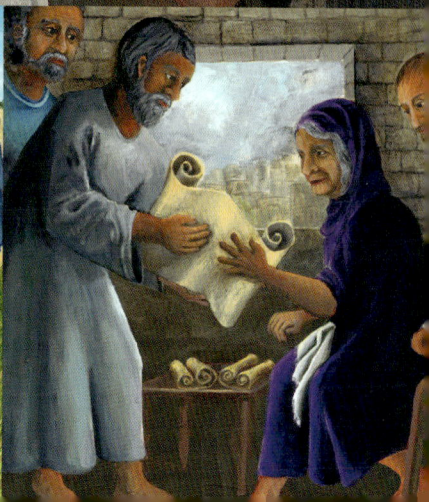

ABIGAIL'S STORY

'You may not look like a prophet – but you do sound like one.'

I sighed, 'I realise now that that isn't very important … I just wish they'd listen to me.'

Shallum smiled at me, 'If God himself came to speak to them, I'm not entirely sure they'd listen.'

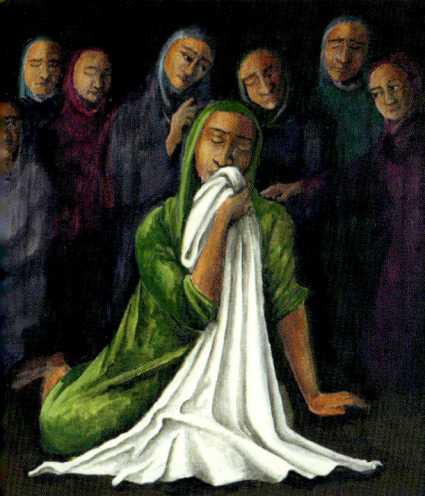

NOTES
AND
RESOURCES

Sarah's Story

Bible passage(s)

Genesis 18.1-15 – and, if you want to get a sense of the broad sweep of the Abraham and Sarah story, Genesis 11.27—12.20 and 15.1—17.8

For reflection

- One of the points I was trying to draw out in the story was how hard it might have been for Sarah to hear of Abraham's conversations with God, but not to encounter God herself until the Lord appeared at the Oaks of Mamre. Abraham is praised for his faith, but what might this have felt like for Sarah?
- However we understand the ages recorded in the story, the point of them is that Abraham and Sarah had to wait a very long time for God's promises to be fulfilled, without knowing if they ever would be. Waiting is never easy to do. What have you learned about waiting in your life?
- Think about laughter. What different kinds of laughter are there? Could laughter be important for us spiritually?

It might help you to know ...

Dates for Abraham and Sarah

One of the hotly contested areas of discussion in Old Testament scholarship is whether it is possible to give a date for Abraham and Sarah. Those that try to provide a date can only do so in the most general of terms and point to the late third millennium or second millennium BC. According to Genesis, when God called Abram in Genesis 12.4 Abram was seventy-five. Ishmael was born when he was eighty-six and Isaac when he was one hundred.

According to Genesis 17.17, Sarah was ten years younger than Abraham and so was ninety when Isaac was born. Although there is, obviously, much discussion about how seriously to take the ages given in the text, in this story I take them at face value for the sake of clarity and ease.

The cities of Ur and Haran

The city of Ur used to be a coastal city on the bank of the Euphrates, though is now far inland. Its rich cultural history can be traced back far into ancient history to the early third millennium BC, and archaeological remains indicate that it had a vibrant urban culture even then.

Haran is around 700 miles from Ur and is thought to be in modern-day Turkey. Although the two names 'Haran' – son of Terah – and 'Haran' – the place Terah moves to – look the same in English, they are different in Hebrew. The name Haran is pronounced with a soft 'h'; the placename has a hard 'h' like the 'ch' in Bach, so would sound different. The similarity of the two words, nevertheless, is striking and not explained by the text itself, especially not in English where they look the same.

Names and their meanings

Much is made in Genesis 17 about the meaning of Abram/ Abraham and Sarai/Sarah's names. The problem is that it is all a bit more complicated than appears on the surface.

Ab-ram means in Hebrew 'father of Exaltation' but the change to 'Ab-raham' is less clear and there isn't a word for multitude that matches the form given in Genesis 17. The change from Sarai to Sarah might indicate a change from 'my princess' to 'the princess', but even that isn't completely clear. What seems to be most important is that God changed their names, not what they meant after he had done so.

What is clear, however, is that the name Isaac (Yitzhak) is connected to the verb 'zahak' – laughs.

Huldah's Story

Bible passage(s)

1 Kings 22.1-20

The reference made by Shallum in the story was to an episode in Hezekiah's life which can be found in 2 Kings 20.12-19.

For reflection

- One of the themes that runs through a lot of prophecy is the theme of whether people listen to what is being said or not. What prevents us from listening to hard things, whether prophetic or otherwise?
- What are we – as a society as a whole – refusing to listen to today? What voices are you as an individual reluctant to listen to?
- Who are our prophets today?

It might help you to know …

Huldah and her family

Although not well known, Huldah is one of the few female prophets in the Bible. Others who are called prophets include Miriam [Exodus 15.20]; Deborah [Judges 4.4]; Noadiah [Nehemiah 6.14]; 'the prophetess' [Isaiah 8.3]; Anna [Luke 2.25-27]; and, less positively, 'the woman who calls herself a prophet' [Revelation 2.18]. Long after Huldah's life, gates leading into the Temple were named after her.

Not much is known about Huldah beyond what is

contained in 2 Kings 22. Jewish tradition associates her with a relative of Jeremiah (Megillah 14b) and Jeremiah 32.7 refers to an uncle of Jeremiah's called 'Shallum', which is the same name as Huldah husband. The idea that Huldah was Jeremiah's aunt is a nice one, so I refer to it in the story.

Shallum is identified in 2 Kings 22.14 as the keeper of the wardrobe. This would have been a job undertaken by a Levite, whose role it would have been to care for the priestly garments from the Temple.

The Book of the Law

Scholars generally agree that the Book of the Law found in the Temple was the Book of Deuteronomy, or at least an early version of it. Where it came from and why it was there in the Temple is not known, but the story of 1 and 2 Samuel and 1 and 2 Kings tells of many kings ignoring the law and doing what they wanted to do instead. The romantic idea of Josiah finding an old and dusty copy of the law and using it to reform the worship of God is what lies behind the reforms that are described in 2 Kings 22 and 23.

The implication of these reforms is that Josiah did listen to the word of the Lord that came to Huldah in this story which, arguably, makes her one of the more successful prophets in the Old Testament.

Abigail's Story

Bible passage
Luke 1.5-25

For reflection

- The Temple was thought of as the 'gateway to Heaven' – a place where God's presence would be more likely to be encountered than in other places. Are there places that you think of as places where you a more likely to encounter God?

- Why do you think Zechariah was struck dumb after he met the angel? It's an odd feature of the story, as Mary seems to have been as surprised by the angel's message to her as Zechariah was, but she wasn't struck dumb in the same way.

- The phrase 'the Lord's favour' or 'God's favour' appears over and over again throughout the Bible. We take it as a positive thing, but many stories imply that God's favour turns people's lives upside down and inside out. How would you interpret 'God's favour' as a phrase?

It might help you to know …

Priests in the Temple

During the reigns of David and Solomon, the descendants of Aaron were split into twenty-four sections. The eighth of these was the section of Abijah. All priests would serve in the Temple for the three main festivals – Passover, Pentecost and Tabernacles – and for the rest of the time they would live somewhere in Israel and would return for a week's service once every six months (i.e. they would serve in the Temple for two weeks a year plus the three festivals). As they would have been literate, it is thought that for the rest of their time they would have acted as scribes in the places where they lived.

Temple service

Numbers 8.23-26 gives the age that a Levite can serve in what was then the Tabernacle as twenty-five (with an upper limit of fifty). 1 Chronicles 23.27 states that David reduced this to twenty. It is assumed that a similar age range was given for Priests as well.

Between them, the Priests and Levites looked after both the Temple building and the worship that took place within it. This involved duties ranging from animal sacrifice through to cleaning and upkeep of the Temple. It is hard to be sure exactly which duties fell to the Priests and which to the Levites, though the Levites appear to have been Temple musicians and gatekeepers to the Temple. Only the High Priest could enter the Holy of Holies, and only then on the Day of Atonement. But a priest would enter the Holy Place (the area in front of the Holy of Holies) to burn incense and pray twice a day. Luke implies that they were chosen by lot to do this.

The casting of lots

The garments of the High Priest are described in detail in Exodus 28. They include the Ephod and the Breastplate which together seem to have formed a container for the

Urim and Thummim. It isn't entirely clear how the Urim and Thummim were used to make decisions, but the description I give in the story seems to be the closest we can get. It would be a cumbersome task twice a day, so it may not have happened like this every day. As with other details in these stories, however, I am taking what the biblical text says at face value.

Mary's Story

Bible passages
Luke 1.26-37
Matthew 1.18-25

For reflection

- How much do you think Mary and Joseph understood about Jesus and who he would be?
- What inspires you most about the character of Mary?
- I was struck when reflecting on Mary as I wrote this story, how much we project onto her about who she was and what she thought. It doesn't mean we shouldn't do this, but it is helpful to be aware of what we are doing. What do you think are some of the key 'projections' we make onto Mary?

It might help you to know …

Anna and Joachim in Sepphoris

Christian tradition names Mary's parents as Anna (or Anne) and Joachim and locates their home in Sepphoris, a large market town four miles north of Nazareth. Archaeologists have found large numbers of storage jars in the region which they think were made in Shikhin, a village next to the town. Even though Sepphoris is not mentioned in the New Testament, it was an important settlement during the time of Jesus, known particularly for its trade.

Houses in Nazareth

Archaeology of Nazareth in the first century suggests that houses from the period were half-hewn into the caves of hillside and built outwards from there. A recent discovery of a first-century dwelling in Nazareth (underneath the Sisters of Nazareth convent in the middle of Nazareth) reveals a very simple house with a just a few rooms, built outwards from a cave in the hillside. This would have meant that the house would have been cool in the summer months and dimly lit all year round.

Census

One of the great conundrums of the story of Jesus' birth is the mention of the census by Luke. There are various problems with it. There is no Roman record of a census for the whole empire, and there is no record of people needing to move to their hometown for a census when they did take place. The census Luke seems to have in mind was the census of the region of Judea by the Governor Quirinius, when the Romans took over the territory from Herod Archelaus in AD 6, which subsequently caused a riot. As Herod the Great died in 4 BC, it is hard to see how the reference to Herod in Matthew's Gospel and the census in Luke's Gospel marry up. I decided, therefore, in these stories, to attribute the movement of Joseph and Mary to Bethlehem to rumours that were heard rather than an actual census. There are numerous other solutions to the problem, but this one worked in these stories.

Shiphrah's Story

Bible passage
Luke 2.1-7

For reflection

- Does it make any difference to your imagining of the story, if Mary and Joseph were not alone for the birth of Jesus but had other people with them?
- What might people who lived elsewhere in Bethlehem have noticed when Jesus was born? Do you imagine they would have seen the angels? Would they have noticed the shepherds arriving?
- What for you are the most important details in the story of Jesus' birth? Why are they important for you?

It might help you to know …

The 'inn'

Christian tradition – and countless nativity plays – portray Jesus being born in a stable. The problem is that the text is far from clear that he was. All it says was that he was laid in a feeding trough, because there was no room in the '*kataluma*.' The word traditionally translated 'inn' is thought by many New Testament scholars to be better translated as 'guest room' or 'upper room'. It is used again at the end of Jesus' ministry to refer to the upper room in which Jesus shared a last supper with his friends. The more usual word for inn is *pandocheion*, which is the word used for the place that the Samaritan took the injured man in Jesus' parable of the Good Samaritan

Many houses in places like Bethlehem would have had an area downstairs where livestock could be kept overnight. The reference to a *kataluma* therefore suggests that the room – or space – set aside for guests was full, and so Jesus was placed in a feeding trough downstairs in the house where Mary and Joseph were staying. This is the image I had in my mind while I was writing the story.

Midwifery and the ancient world

Midwives exist in cultures throughout the world. Often not medically trained, the midwife would be the person in the town or village who had years of skill of delivering babies and who would be called to help a young woman when a baby was on the way. I enjoyed playing with the idea of there being another, more experienced woman present as Mary gave birth, and wondering what it felt like for her to deliver the Saviour of the world.

The two most famous midwives in the Bible are Shiphrah and Puah, mentioned in Exodus 1.15 as the midwives who saved countless babies after the Egyptian decree that all Israelite boy babies should be killed at birth.

Rachel's Story

Bible passages

Matthew 2.13-18

Luke 2.8-20

For reflection

- Why do you think Matthew included this brutal story in his story of Jesus' birth? What was he trying to communicate with it?
- What might it have felt like to have lived in Bethlehem on the periphery of the events surrounding Jesus' birth? What might you have thought about what was going on?
- What do you think the importance of the shepherds is in Luke's story? (See the note below for more exploration of this.)

It might help you to know …

Shepherds

A lot is said about shepherds at Christmas time. They are often contrasted with the wise men from Mathew's Gospel, with the wise men held up as powerful and wealthy and the shepherds as poor and on the edges of society. This may be the right contrast to draw, but the term 'shepherd' is a broad one and used in different ways throughout the Bible. The word can be used of wealthy landowners who own many sheep, as well as jobbing, hired hands who slept out on the hillside to look after the flock. The question is what the significance of the shepherds is in the story, and Luke doesn't help the reader to identify this. This could mean that the shepherds had multiple resonances – reminding us of David, being in a place where it is easy to see the sky, etc. We perhaps also assume that these shepherds were middle-aged men, roughened by years sleeping outside. In fact, the Bible most often refers to teenagers as shepherd boys (or indeed girls). Examples of people like Rachel (Genesis 29.6) and Zipporah (Exodus 2.16) who were looking after their father's flocks suggest that girls also looked after sheep before they were married.

Rachel's tomb

Genesis 35.16-21 recounts Rachel's death in childbirth, giving birth to a son whom she called 'son of my sorrow' (Ben-oni) but whom Jacob renamed 'son of my right hand' (Ben-jammin). She was buried, the text says, near Ephrath (in other words, Bethlehem), and although there are numerous sites associated with her tomb, the most famous is the one just north of Bethlehem. There is no tradition of the tomb making an eerie sound as the wind blows (I made that up), but it felt important to introduce Rachel's weeping into the story as something other than just an idea.

The quotation mentioned in the story comes from the book of Jeremiah 31.15 and recounts Rachel weeping for her descendants as they were taken into exile. Matthew picks up it and uses it again in the story of the slaughter of the innocents.

Elizabeth's Story

Bible passage

Luke 1.39-45 and 57-66

For reflection

- What do you imagine Mary and Elizabeth talked about when they met, while both were pregnant?
- Various stories in the Bible remind us that attitudes to childbirth have changed dramatically since the first century, when the inability to conceive was seen as a punishment from God. How do we tell these stories responsibly today, in a such a way that does not perpetuate the idea that a woman without a child is 'barren'?
- Why do you think names are so important in the Bible?

It might help you to know ...

Where Elizabeth and Zechariah lived.

Luke simply states that Mary visited Elizabeth in the 'hill country'. Christian tradition has identified this as a place called Ein Kerem, a village to the west of Jerusalem. It would have been a convenient place for a priest to live while he waited for his service of God in the Temple twice a year.

Names

Much is made in the story of John the Baptist of the importance of giving a son his father's name. It is hard to tell how important this was in practice. I have used it as a lever for this story, but whether there was a widespread expectation that a son would be given his father's name in this period is hard to tell from the evidence available.

Mariamne's Story

Bible passage
Matthew 2.1-12

For reflection

- Herod's rage at the birth of Jesus tells us a lot about his insecurity as a ruler. He did everything to cling onto a power he didn't really have. In contrast, Jesus gave up power he had out of love for the world. What does this teach us about power and how we relate to it? (Hint: there isn't an easy answer to this, or at least not one that is easy to live out!)

- In the NRSV Bible translation, the word used in Matthew 2.8 and 11 to describe what the Magi did when they saw Jesus is translated as 'pay him homage'; in the King James Version it is translated as 'worshipped'. The same word can mean both. What do you think they did? Does it matter either way?

It might help you to know …

Herod the Great and Mariamne

Some think that Herod the Great was a brilliant ruler who was both canny and resourceful; others think he was an insecure despot desperate to cling onto power at all costs. The reality is he could have been both, but the story told about him in the New Testament suggests more of the latter view of Herod.

I chose to focus the story around Herod's wife at the

time of the birth of Jesus, as the story about her marriage to Herod does seem to support a view of Herod as insecure and haunted by power. Herod divorced his first wife, Doris, when he was made king and married a Hasmonean princess called Mariamne. She was a great beauty, and it is clear Herod loved her. They were married in 37 BC, but their relationship was stormy and eventually Herod had her executed in 29 BC, fearing that she would challenge his power.

A few years later, Herod heard of the beautiful daughter of Simon Boethus, a priest from Alexandria, who was also called Mariamne. He decided to marry her to help him get over his grief but couldn't do so because her father was too low born. So Herod made him High Priest and later married Mariamne II in 24 BC. In 4 BC, shortly before his death, Herod learned of a plot to overthrow him instigated by Queen Doris' sons. He also learned that Mariamne II knew about the plot but hadn't told him. As a result, she was banished from the palace.

Following Herod the Great's death, the kingdom was split between some of his sons: Herod Archaelaus (Judea), Herod Antipas (Galilee) and Philip the Tetrarch (Iturea). Herod Antipas' second wife was Herodias, who was the daughter of another of Herod the Great's sons (Aristobulus IV) and had previously been married to Herod II, her half-uncle. Her daughter Salome – who famously danced for the head of John the Baptist – married her uncle, Philip the Tetrarch. This illustrates the profoundly messy relationships among the Herodians and why John the Baptist was so vehement in his criticism of them.

Anna's Story

Bible passage
Luke 2.22-38

For reflection

- One of the fascinating features of the story of the Presentation of Jesus in the Temple is the fact that Simeon and Anna both recognized who Jesus was, even though he was a baby. What was it, do you think, that made them recognize him?

- Luke says that Simeon came to the Temple guided by the Spirit and Anna was there because she was a prophet and never left the Temple. How do these two contrast with each other? Is there anything to learn from this?

- What signs of God in the world do you notice? What leads you to think they are signs of God?

It might help you to know ...

Anna, the prophet

As we noted with Huldah, Anna is one of the few women in the Bible who is identified as a prophet. Luke tells us no more about why she was called a prophet, but it is interesting that she is one of the few people in the Gospels themselves who is called a prophet.

Luke's description of her is slightly confusing. It says that she had lived with her husband for seven years and then as a widow either to the age of eighty-four, or as a widow for eighty-four years. I decided to go with the latter to emphasize her great age which allows me to bookend these nine stories with two women of great age – Sarah and Anna – who had to wait for a long time for something. Sarah waited for a baby and so did Anna, but the baby was not hers.

I have also assumed that Anna had no children. It is possible that a widow with children might live in the Temple rather than with her family, but the fact that she 'never left the Temple but worshiped there with fasting and prayer night and day' does suggest that she has no family to live with. (For one of the stories in *Women of Holy Week* I imagined that Anna had a great-niece who carries her name, and who also encounters Jesus in the Temple.)

In a string of stories which often have childbirth as their focus, it feels somehow appropriate to end with a childless woman who, unusually for the New Testament, is named and remembered as a prophet. Although Luke's account about her is brief, she looms large in my mind as a symbol of all the women we have reflected on through Advent and Christmas: a woman of courage and vision; of patience and persistence; of love and joy. We remember her because of a fleeting moment in her life, but she was ready for that moment because of the faithfulness with which she lived the eighty-four (or so) years before that moment.

I dedicate this book to the very many women – some I know, and many I don't – whose lives are likewise lived in long faithfulness to the God of love.

Women of Holy Week

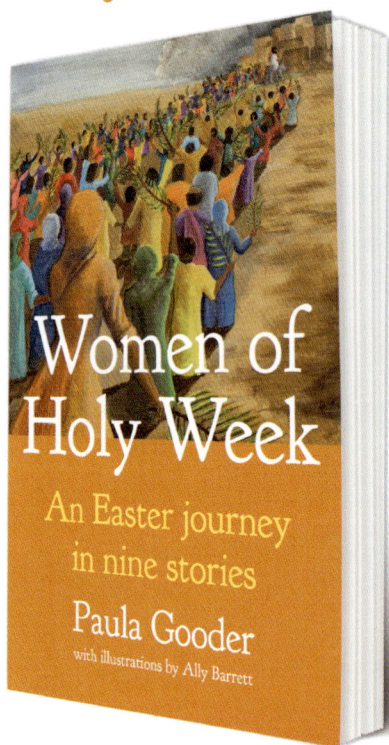

Women of Holy Week

An Easter journey in nine stories

Paula Gooder

with illustrations by Ally Barrett

An Easter journey in nine stories

✝ CHURCH HOUSE
PUBLISHING